~➤ BOOK TWO ←~

SEPRON
THE SEA SERPENT

ADAM BLADE

ILLUSTRATED BY EZRA TUCKER

A
LITTLE APPLE
PAPERBACK

SCHOLASTIC INC.

New York Toronto London Auckland Sydney
Mexico City New Delhi Hong Kong Buenos Aires

With thanks to Cherith Baldry
To James Noble

No part of this publication may be reproduced, stored in a retrieval system, or transmitted in any form or by any means, electronic, mechanical, photocopying, recording, or otherwise, without written permission of the publisher. For information regarding permission, write to Working Partners Ltd., 1 Albion Place, London, W6OQT, United Kingdom.

ISBN-13: 978-0-439-90654-8
ISBN-10: 0-439-90654-7

Beast Quest series created by Working Partners Ltd, London.
BEAST QUEST is a registered trademark of Working Partners Ltd.

Copyright © 2007 by Working Partners Ltd.

All rights reserved. Published by Scholastic Inc., 557 Broadway, New York, NY 10012, by arrangement with Working Partners Ltd.

SCHOLASTIC, LITTLE APPLE and associated logos are trademarks and/or registered trademarks of Scholastic Inc.

12 11 10 9 8 7 6 5 4 3 2 1   7 8 9 10 11 12/0

Designed by Tim Hall
Printed in the U.S.A.   40
First printing, March 2007

Reader,

Welcome to Avantia. I am Aduro — a good wizard residing in the palace of King Hugo. You join us at a difficult time. Let me explain. . . .

It is laid down in the Ancient Scripts that the peaceful kingdom of Avantia would one day be plunged into danger by the evil wizard, Malvel.

That time has come.

Under Malvel's evil spell, six Beasts — fire dragon, sea serpent, mountain giant, night mare, ice beast, and winged flame — run wild and destroy the land they once protected.

The kingdom is in great danger.

The Scripts also predict an unlikely hero. They say that a boy shall take up the Quest to free the beasts and save the kingdom.

We hope this young boy will take up the Quest. Will you join us as we wait and watch?

Avantia salutes you,
Aduro

⇥ Prologue ⇤

Calum loosened the rope and let the sail down. The fishing boat rocked gently on the waves. His father, Matt, began to cast the net out, whistling softly through his teeth as he worked.

"I don't know why we bother," he grumbled. "We haven't caught any fish in weeks."

"They say there's something out here," Calum replied, scanning the vast sea. "A sea monster that has scared the fish away."

Matt dismissed the idea with a snort. "That's just an old wives' tale."

Calum kept eyeing the horizon. Nothing broke

the surface of the steel gray waters except for a steep, rocky islet not far from the beach.

"I'm not so sure," he said. "Uncle Hal told me he saw a dark shape in the water last time he took his boat out. 'Something big,' he said."

"Driftwood or seaweed most likely." Matt snorted again. "Here, son, give me a hand with this rope."

Calum and Matt hauled the net in. It was empty.

"Useless," said Matt.

He cast the net out again. As Calum watched it sink into the depths of the water, he spotted something between the boat and the shore. It looked as if the sea was boiling. It churned and foamed, causing waves to crash against the sides of their boat.

"Look!" he cried, pointing. "Over there!"

Matt turned, grabbing the edge of the boat as it started to rock dangerously. Out of the sea rose a monstrous head with a long, slender neck. Its thick scales were covered with barnacles and seawater streamed down its sides. A collar around the serpent's neck glinted in the sunshine.

Matt let out a yell. "What is it?"

Calum scrambled for the rope to raise the sail, but it was too late. The beast's neck arched, its giant head looming over the boat. Calum stared up into its cold eyes. Choking with terror, he saw the creature's jaws gape open, a forked tongue emerged through rows of razor-sharp teeth. In a swift motion, the beast brought its head down and clamped its jaws shut. Its teeth snapped the boat's mast and sent splinters down on Calum and Matt like rain.

Seawater sloshed over Calum as the boat smashed around him. Cowering, he wrapped his arms around his head. He squeezed his eyes shut tight in fear as the roaring of the sea monster echoed all around him.

And then, all of a sudden, everything became eerily silent.

→ CHAPTER ONE ←

THE ROAD TO THE WEST

Tom brought Storm to a halt at the foot of a rocky slope. He and Elenna slid to the ground so that the horse could rest. Silver the wolf flopped down beside them and let his tongue loll out as he panted.

The hill where they had met Ferno the Fire Dragon had vanished into the distance. Now Tom and Elenna were heading westward on the next stage of their Beast Quest.

Tom's heart began thumping as he remembered how they had freed Ferno. It had been a dangerous mission and Tom felt lucky to have survived unscathed.

"I can't believe you leaped up on his wing!" Elenna said, guessing what Tom was thinking about.

"It wouldn't have helped much if you hadn't shot that arrow up to me with the key tied to it," Tom replied. "I'd never have gotten his collar off without that."

"What you did was still the bravest thing I've ever seen," Elenna insisted.

"We *both* freed Ferno," Tom said firmly. "And now Avantia will have water again." Tom grinned as he remembered the way Ferno, once he was free, had smashed the rocks that were damming the river.

While Tom was remembering their first adventure, Silver leaped up and let out an impatient yelp.

Elenna turned to Tom, a determined look in her eyes. "We'd better push on," she said.

Tom could still hear the words of the Wizard

Aduro echoing in his ears. The dark magic of Malvel had turned all the Beasts of Avantia evil. Freeing Ferno the Fire Dragon was only the first of his tasks. Excitement and anticipation bubbled up inside Tom as he recalled Aduro's words — that it was his duty to save his people. But he had doubts, too. He was still just a young blacksmith's apprentice, after all. And there was so much he had to do — so many Beasts to conquer!

He'd been waiting his entire life for this adventure, and even though he didn't know where his father was, Tom was determined to make him proud.

"Let's have another look at the map," he said.

He pulled out the magic scroll that Aduro had given him before he left the King's palace. One path on it glowed green, winding through hills and woodlands until it reached the sea in the West.

As Tom looked at the map, a serpent's head reared out of the waves drawn on the paper. A jagged tail slapped down, sending spray high into the air. Tom started as a drop splashed onto his hand.

"There's Sepron," said Elenna, her voice filled with awe. Aduro had told them all about their next Beast.

"I still can't believe it!" said Tom. "A sea serpent!"

"He looks angry." Elenna's eyes were wide as she realized the huge task in front of them. "What do you think he might do?"

"Whatever it is, we're going to stop him," Tom said boldly. "That's the next part of our quest."

Silver let out another loud yelp. He grabbed the corner of Elenna's cloak in his teeth and tugged gently. At the foot of the slope, Storm scraped one hoof impatiently on the stones.

Tom laughed. "All right, I know. It's time to move on."

He checked the map one last time and stowed it away in his pocket. Before he scrambled back onto

Storm, he made sure that the shield Aduro had given him was safely stowed in his saddlebag. The dragon scale shone in its slot on the shield's rough surface. *Was it true,* Tom wondered, *that the shield would now protect them from fire?*

He swung himself onto the saddle. Elenna sprang up behind him and wrapped her arms around his waist. Tom patted Storm's glossy, black neck.

"Forward!" he cried. "On to the West!"

At first, the path zigzagged up the slope, then through a strand of trees. By the time the sun went down, they had reached a pass winding through a range of low hills.

Tom halted beside a stream and slid to the ground. "This would be a good place to make camp," he decided.

Elenna helped him take off Storm's bridle so the horse could drink from the stream. Silver stood beside him, lapping thirstily. Tom was hungry and thirsty himself and scooped a handful of cool water into his mouth. Then he started to collect sticks for a fire.

"I'm starving!" said Elenna. "I'll see if there are any nuts or berries on these bushes."

While she was searching, Storm feasted on the grass beside the path.

"What about Silver?" asked Tom.

"He can find something for himself," Elenna replied. "Go on, boy, but come back soon."

Silver disappeared among the rocks, his bushy tail wagging. He returned before Tom and Elenna had finished eating, and they all settled down for the night. Tom looked up at the stars, thinking about Sepron. He hoped they could reach the coast soon, before the sea monster could do any more damage.

When they set off again the next morning, they soon reached the edge of the hills. A long, smooth slope led down to the valley before them. In the

distance, Tom could make out the glimmer of the sea.

"We're almost there!" Elenna exclaimed.

A flash of light on the water caught Tom's eye. He let out a gasp.

"What's the matter?" Elenna asked.

"I'm not sure . . . I think I saw Sepron."

He felt Elenna's grip on him tighten. "Where?"

"Over there, near that tall rock." Tom pointed. "But he's gone now."

He swung himself onto Storm's back and urged him on. They rode down the hill and into the valley. The path led them through farmland. Everything seemed deserted. Great patches of ground were covered in burned stubble.

"Look!" Elenna cried, pointing to the blackened timbers of what had been a farmhouse. "The dragon was here."

A chill ran down Tom's spine, even though he knew that Ferno was free now and would never again blast the land with his fire. He urged Storm to a faster trot, eager to keep moving. Silver bounded a few paces ahead, his tongue lolling out.

Then, without warning, Storm reared. His forelegs pawed the air. Elenna let out a cry of alarm and gripped Tom harder to stop herself from sliding off.

"Storm — steady!" Tom yelled.

When the horse's forelegs returned to the ground, he began skittering to one side. Tom tugged on the reins but couldn't get the horse under control. Then he noticed that Silver was standing still, his legs stiff and the bushy gray fur on his shoulders bristling. He began whining uneasily.

"Something's wrong," said Elenna. Tom glanced back at her and saw alarm in her eyes. "They can sense it."

Tom looked all around. He couldn't see anything but empty land. There was no sign of danger. But

Silver kept on whining. Storm was tossing his head, his eyes darting back and forth in panic. Beads of sweat rolled down his black coat.

"What is it, boy?" Tom was still struggling to keep the terrified horse on the path. "What's the matter?"

Silver let out a deep growl. He was staring straight ahead. Following his gaze, Tom thought he could make something out on the horizon. It looked as if the farmland was moving. Taking a closer look, Tom saw that it was a muddy torrent of water. He watched as it churned and frothed, swallowing up the land as it rushed closer to where they stood.

"Tom," Elenna said, her voice choking with fear. "It's a tidal wave!"

CHAPTER TWO

RACE AGAINST THE SEA

FOR AN INSTANT, TOM FROZE.

"Tom!" Elenna tugged hard at his elbow.

Wrenching on the reins, Tom brought Storm's head around and dug his heels into the horse's flank. "Run!" he yelled.

Storm leaped forward like an arrow from a bow. Growling fiercely, Silver raced along not far behind.

"Faster!" Elenna cried. "The water is catching up."

Tom risked a glance over his shoulder. The dark water was surging closer. He couldn't believe how fast it was coming.

He bent low over the stallion's neck. "Come on, Storm," he urged. "You can do it!"

They raced along the path toward higher ground. Glancing back, he saw that Elenna's face was white with terror. Beyond her, the flood nipped at their heels. They could feel the water's cold spray. The hills where they would be safe were too far away. They weren't going to make it.

Just then, Elenna tugged at Tom's shoulder. "Over there!" she yelled, pointing to one side.

Tom saw an outcropping of rocks to their left. A smooth slab of stone covered in moss stood high above the flat valley. It just might be high enough for them to get safely out of the way. Tom pulled on Storm's reins and the horse plunged away from the path. His hooves thundered across the blackened fields.

The murky water was gaining on them. Storm's pace slowed as he began to climb, struggling over the rough ground. Tom had to cling to the front of the saddle to keep his seat. Elenna's arms were so tight around his waist that he could hardly breathe. He couldn't see Silver, though he heard the wolf howling.

As the slope grew steeper, Tom glanced back. The wave was still close on their heels. Up ahead was a ledge where they'd be safe, if only they could get there before the frothing water swallowed them.

"Faster, Storm!" he gasped.

The stallion gave a final burst of speed, his hooves clattering on bare rock. Tom let out a yell of panic. If Storm slipped, they would all drown in the dark, churning water.

Just as Storm leaped onto the ledge, the water surged forward, smashing against the wall. A wave of thick, muddy water crashed over them. Below, the flood swirled and lapped at their feet.

Tom and Elenna slid to the ground, dripping with dark, dirty water.

Storm was sweating and trembling. Tom patted

his neck. "Well done, boy. You saved us. You're the bravest —"

"Where's Silver?" Elenna's cry interrupted him.

Tom looked out over the valley of churning water. A branch bobbed roughly on the surface before disappearing under the water. Everywhere Tom looked, debris swirled in the flood. But there was no sign of the wolf.

"Silver! Silver!" Elenna called frantically.

A faint yelp answered her. Tom spotted a dark shape thrusting through the waves. Silver was paddling furiously toward them. His muzzle vanished under the swirling water, then reappeared. Tom couldn't tell if he was making any headway.

"He can't do it! He'll drown!" Elenna sobbed.

She began wrenching off her boots, ready to plunge into the water.

Tom clutched her arm. "No — it's too dangerous! You'll drown, too."

Before Elenna could struggle free, a rush of water

tossed Silver closer. His paws churned, bringing him within their reach. With a gasp of relief, Elenna leaned over the edge and grabbed his collar.

With her help, Silver scrambled to safety. He was panting hard, and water streamed off his thick coat. Elenna knelt down and hugged him.

After a moment, she stood up. "We're safe," she said, looking out at the receding flood.

"That was close." Tom nodded. "Now I'm *sure* I caught a glimpse of Sepron back there. He must have caused the tidal wave. If we don't free him, he'll drown the whole western kingdom."

Tom gritted his teeth. He knew he had to free Sepron — no matter how dangerous it would be. This was his quest, and nothing could make him give up.

CHAPTER THREE

STRANDED

TOM PULLED THE MAP OUT OF HIS POCKET. THE glowing green path that had led to the western coast now ended in a waste of water. The spike of rock where he'd spotted Sepron earlier was the only landmark left.

Tom rolled up the map and looked around. In front of him, the floodwaters had slowly begun to recede, leaving behind a wasteland of mud and debris. Behind him, a rough slope led up to the ridge. A couple of twisted thorn trees stood out against the sky.

"It'll be impossible to cross the valley now," Tom realized. "The mud is too thick."

"Maybe we can get back into the hills," Elenna suggested. "There *must* be a way around."

Tom pointed to the ridge. "We should be able to see from up there."

With Elenna beside him, he climbed the slope. When Tom reached the thorn trees, he stopped in horror.

"No!" Elenna exclaimed.

The valley below them was completely destroyed. What had been rolling farmland before was now a lake of mud and debris. Almost nothing was left standing. Everywhere they looked, it was total devastation. The lower part of the ridge had disappeared underwater. Now they were stranded on a peninsula with no way to get back to the hills — or out to the sea.

Elenna folded her arms and let out a sigh. "*Now* what do we do?"

Tom gazed out toward the West. Out to sea he could still see the rocky islet poking out of the water. But without a boat, they had no way of getting there.

Would they have to stay stranded here until the mud dried and the valley became passable again?

"What's that over there?" Elenna pointed down the ridge, to a clump of trees near the waterline.

Behind the trees, Tom could make out the gray walls of buildings, and he caught a glimpse of movement. "There's someone down there," he said.

"Let's go and see," Elenna suggested. "They might need help."

"Good idea."

Before they could go and investigate, Tom and Elenna went to collect Silver and Storm.

Silver was still resting after his struggles. As they drew close to him he scrambled to his feet and shook himself vigorously, spattering them with drops of muddy water. Elenna rumpled his ears.

Tom went over to Storm and rubbed his nose.

"Not far now, boy," he promised. "Then you can have a proper rest."

Leading the tired horse, he made his way down the ridge. Elenna followed with Silver at her heels.

As they drew nearer, Tom saw a group of people gathered around three or four stone cottages. Some were sitting on the ground, their heads buried in their hands. Others just stared out toward the sea. Children were clinging to their mothers and somewhere a baby was wailing.

Lower down the slope, there were more cottages, all partly covered by water. The sea was washing in and out through the windows. Beyond them, Tom could see only thatched roofs, then nothing but unbroken sea.

Elenna halted, her eyes wide with shock. "It's a village!" she exclaimed. "The water has covered most of it."

"I hope no one was hurt," said Tom. Anger and

anxiety flooded over him as he thought of the destruction Sepron had caused, all because of Malvel's evil spell.

Tom and Elenna hurried toward the water. As they drew closer they had to wade through the wreckage: shattered pieces of wood, fallen trees, and strands of seaweed. In the mud, Elenna spotted something glimmering in the sunlight — unharmed and beautiful. It was a long, slender knife with a pearl handle.

"Come on!" Tom called out.

Elenna stooped to pick up the knife. "All right, I'm coming."

At the sound of their voices, a boy standing at the water's edge turned and saw them. He was tall and red-haired with a freckled face.

"My knife!" he called out. "I can't believe you found it!"

"It's beautiful," Elenna said, handing it back to

him. "You're lucky it survived. I'm Elenna," she added, "and this is Tom."

"I'm Calum. And I'm lucky *I* survived," said the boy. "I never thought I'd see this again. It's been in our family for ages. We're fisherfolk here, but—"

He broke off as an older man, with gray hair and beard, came trudging toward them. His shoulders drooped and his face was lined with wrinkles.

"This is my father, Matt," said Calum.

Matt looked from Tom to Elenna and back again. "We'd do more to welcome you if we had anything to give you," he said. "But you see how it is."

"Everyone's safe, thank goodness," Calum said. "But look at our village!" He pointed toward the submerged cottages. "What are we going to do now?"

"We'll stay and help," Elenna said.

Calum clenched his fists in anger. "Thanks, but what good can anyone do? We can't live here anymore. We'll have to move away, and it's all the fault of the sea serpent."

"The sea serpent!" Tom exclaimed, exchanging a startled look with Elenna.

"You must think we're talking rubbish," Matt said. "I thought that myself once. But now I've seen the creature. It's out there."

Tom's stomach churned with anticipation. They were in the right place, alright. With a bit of luck, he would soon be able to face Sepron and set him free.

"We were out at sea when we saw it," Calum explained. "It burst out of the water and smashed our boat to pieces. I thought we would drown for sure. But then it vanished as quickly as it had appeared."

"What did you do?" Elenna asked.

"We hung onto scraps of the wreckage and swam ashore," Calum replied. "The whole time I thought the sea serpent would come back any minute and swallow us."

"We're lucky to be alive," Matt finished. "And that wasn't the first bit of trouble, either. For weeks, we've caught next to nothing. Our nets were torn to bits. And now this." He heaved a sigh. "It's no use. We'll have to pack up, all of us, and move farther inland."

"But what will you do? You're fishermen," Tom said. If every fisherman thought like this, how would the Kingdom survive?

Matt snorted. "We *were* fishermen. But there's nothing left to catch, and now all our boats have been washed away. Now we're just beggars."

Tom felt anger growing inside him, but he tried not to let it show. Even though the villagers had survived, their lives had been ruined. He *had* to free Sepron—and soon.

"There's a boat over there." Elenna pointed to

where a small fishing boat lay on its side, not far from the edge of the water.

"It's the only one left," said Calum despairingly. "And it's got a hole in it."

"I'll help you mend it if you like," Elenna offered. "My father is a fisherman. He taught me how to do it."

Matt and Calum looked at each other. Matt shook his head doubtfully, but a spark of hope appeared in Calum's eyes.

"We'll mend it, father," Calum said. "At least it's something to do. We shouldn't give up hope yet."

"All right," agreed Matt reluctantly. He trudged down to the water's edge and stood scanning the sea, looking for the serpent.

Tom wished he could reassure Matt, but he couldn't tell anyone about his quest. And he certainly couldn't tell anyone that the Beast was under an evil spell! The most important task at the moment was to mend the boat. Then he and

Elenna could borrow it to row out and find Sepron.

"Let's get started," Elenna said. "We need wood for a fire, and rope and tar to mend the hole."

Calum glanced around. "There's wood scattered all over by the flood," he said, "but it's all wet."

"We'll have to go to higher ground for dry wood," said Tom.

"Okay," agreed Calum. "And I know where to get some tar." He went off and disappeared into one of the cottages.

While Elenna gathered all the dry twigs and leaves she could find, Tom led Storm up to the trees where there was long grass for him to eat. While Storm grazed, Tom collected fallen branches.

Once he had several large pieces of wood, he lashed them together with rope and tied one end to Storm's saddle. Then he led his horse back to the village.

When he returned, Elenna was already heaping

small scraps of wood together to start the fire. Calum came back from the cottage carrying a pot of tar. Over one shoulder, he had a coil of thick rope. Silver followed behind him with another length of rope trailing from his mouth.

Calum set the tar down near Elenna's pile of wood and handed the rope to Tom. "That's the last of the tar," he said quietly, before going to look for more wood.

Tom crouched down. *This isn't fair!* he thought as he started to unravel the rope. The coarse strands tore at his fingertips but it felt good to be doing something.

Elenna knelt down next to a small pile of leaves, twigs, and frayed bits of rope. She wrapped the string of her bow around a small stick and bent over the tinder. She drew the bow back and forth with practiced strokes, and the little pile began to burn. When the fire was ready, Calum brought an armful of bigger branches and laid them on top.

They crackled in the flames. Matt looked on approvingly.

When Tom had finished unravelling the rope, he and Calum turned the boat over so that they could reach the jagged hole in its side. Tom noticed that the oars were lashed together under the seat. At least they were lucky enough to have those. A boat without oars wouldn't be much use.

Under Matt's watchful gaze, Elenna packed the strands of rope into the hole while Tom put the pot on the fire and found a stick to stir the tar. When the tar was bubbling, Tom used a long ladle to scoop some out and carry it over to the boat. Quickly, Elenna used a scrap of driftwood to plaster the hot tar over the rope strands, inside and out.

Suddenly, Tom heard the fire roaring louder and felt a fierce heat on his back. He spun around to see flames shooting up around the pot. Some of the tar must have spilled and fuelled the fire.

"No!" shouted Calum. "That's the last of the tar. If it burns we won't be able to fix the boat!"

But it was too late. Smoke billowed out of the fire and the branches hurled out bubbles of hot resin. Sparks shot into the air, almost landing in the pot of tar. One landed on the ground just beside the boat. Matt stomped on it to put it out.

Everyone flinched back from the fire as it burned fiercely. Tom had to get the flames under control — but how?

⊷ Chapter Four ↢

Fire and Water

Tom glanced around desperately. They needed a water bucket—something to put out the fire. Then, he spotted his shield leaning against a stone cottage. He ran and grabbed it as the flames continued to rage and threaten the last of the tar.

Using his shield as protection, Tom creeped toward the fire. The heat was incredible. Hot resin spat angrily as flames licked the shield. It was all Tom could do to keep the shield in place. The fire was out of control. As Tom got closer, he had to turn his face away from the unbearable heat.

"Quick!" yelled Matt. "Get him some water!"

Calum rushed to the water's edge, filled a bucket

with seawater, and raced back toward Tom. The fire was still raging, but the shield protected them from the worst of the heat and flames.

Tom held the shield in place as Calum poured water on the base of the fire. A cloud of steam rose over them, but the fire barely died down.

"We need more water!" Tom yelled.

Calum nodded. He ran back to the sea and filled his bucket. But as he hurried to pour it on the fire, a flame jumped around the edge of Tom's shield and scorched Calum's hand.

"Owww!" He dropped the bucket and screamed in pain. It was a bad burn, but they still needed more water, and Calum was losing precious seconds. Wrapping his shirt around his hand, Calum dumped the rest of the water over the flames, and rushed to get more.

By the time Calum returned, the fire was finally showing signs of weakening. He poured the final bucket of water on the smouldering coals. It had taken three trips, but they had controlled the blaze.

Tom lowered his shield and surveyed the damage. The tar was still bubbling and boiling from the heat, and most of it was still there.

"We were lucky," Tom said. "It could've been much worse. How's your hand?"

Calum winced, but tried to hide it. "I think it will be okay," he said. "It hurts, but it's not too bad."

Tom looked around. The earth was scorched and steaming all around him. He realized how lucky they were — if the fire had raged for even a few moments longer, the tar would've been destroyed and then . . . it wasn't worth thinking about.

Tom examined his shield. It had been pressed right up against the heat and flames, and there wasn't even a scorch mark on its rough surface. Aduro was right. The dragon scale really was protection against fire!

Looking over his shoulder, Tom saw Calum staring thoughtfully at the shield. Tom's stomach tightened. What would he say if the fisherman's son questioned him? Calum looked back at him. Tom met his gaze steadily, but didn't try to explain.

"Let's get this pot down," Calum said, giving Tom a knowing look. "Then Elenna can finish the repairs."

Tom helped Calum carry the pot of tar over to the boat. As Elenna finished sealing the leak, Tom wondered if Matt would be willing to lend it to them. After all, it was the village's only boat. But Elenna was right; there was no other way to reach Sepron.

He walked over to where Matt was examining Elenna's repairs. "Matt . . ." he began.

The fisherman looked up. "Yes, what is it?"

"May we borrow your boat for a while? We'll take good care of it."

Matt straightened up. "This is the only seaworthy vessel we have left. We need it if we're going to catch anything to eat."

"We'd have to leave Silver and Storm here with you," Elenna said, coming to stand beside Tom. "And you can be sure we'd never do that if we weren't coming back."

Matt shook his head. "I'm not calling you thieves. But anything could happen. There could be an accident or a storm. And the sea serpent is still out there. You could be drowned, and we'd never see you or our boat again."

"But —" Tom protested.

"I'm sorry. The answer is no."

He turned away to help Calum bandage his burned hand. Tom stared after him in frustration.

Elenna tugged at his arm and pretended to draw in the sand as she whispered, "If they won't lend us the boat, we'll just have to borrow it without their permission."

Tom stared at her. "What? We can't do that!"

"But we'll bring it back. Tom, you know that there'll be more floods and destruction if we don't do something about Sepron. These people will starve. We'll be taking the boat for their own good."

Tom nodded slowly, looking out across the sea. "All right." Out there — somewhere — was Sepron. Tom knew he didn't have a choice. Risk angering Matt and his family? Or risk watching the whole western kingdom be devastated by Malvel's evil spell? Tom's chest heaved as he thought about his aunt and uncle back home, the hope they had placed in him. This was his destiny. The evening sun was going down, setting the water aglow in shades of red and orange.

"We'll take the boat and row out at dawn," Tom said.

→ CHAPTER FIVE ←

ON WITH THE QUEST

TOM AND ELENNA SLEPT ROLLED UP IN BLANKETS on the floor of one of the cottages that had escaped the flood. Some of the villagers were crowded in there with them. Tom was careful to choose a spot near the door, so he and Elenna could sneak out without waking anyone.

Tom woke to feel Elenna shaking him by the shoulder.

"Come on!" she whispered. "It's time."

Faint gray light was leaking through the shuttered windows of the cottage. Tom rose to his feet, careful not to break the early morning quiet, and edged open the door. He and Elenna crept outside.

The sky was growing light above the trees on the ridge. Tom could make out the dark shape of Storm grazing farther up the hill. Silver came bounding out of the trees and sniffed at Elenna's hand.

"Shh, boy," she whispered.

Looking around, Tom saw that the water had gone down a little bit in the night. More of the village was visible now, and Tom and Elenna could see the terrible damage Sepron had caused.

Many of the cottages were reduced to heaps of stone. Others were caked with mud from the floodwaters. The boat was where they had left it, but now they would have to carry it to the water's edge.

They both stooped down and gripped the upturned boat at its bow and stern.

"Hey! What do you think you're doing?" Tom

and Elenna froze as a shout came from the cottage they had just left.

Tom let go of the boat and straightened up. Calum was racing toward them with a confused look on his face.

Tom ran to meet him. "Calum, please don't wake the village. We can explain."

Calum's face grew dark with anger. "I saw you whispering yesterday and didn't say anything. I thought you wanted to help us. Now you're trying to steal our boat."

"We only want to borrow it," Elenna protested.

"It's not called borrowing if you don't have permission," Calum said coldly.

Tom hesitated. To his relief, none of the other villagers had been awakened by Calum's shout. If only he could persuade the boy. But he knew that he couldn't tell anyone about the Beast Quest without causing a panic.

"I need the boat for something really important," he began.

Calum no longer looked angry as he gave Tom a thoughtful look. Then he glanced out to sea. "I think I can guess," he said.

"Guess what?" asked Tom.

"You seem like someone with a mission," said Calum. "I had the same feeling about a man who passed through our village about a year ago."

Tom's heartbeat quickened. Could Calum have seen his father? "Was his name Taladon?" he asked, gripping the boy's shoulders.

Calum shook his head. "He didn't say. He just told us he was on a quest." He paused and went on, "I think you might be on a quest, too."

Tom was sure that the stranger must have been his father, Taladon. Tom ached to know more. He wanted to ask about every detail of his stay in the village, but there was no time. The sky was growing brighter and soon the villagers would be getting up. He held the boy's gaze steadily. Elenna didn't say a word, though Silver whined softly.

After a moment, Calum gave a brisk nod. "All right. I'll help you move the boat."

The three of them lifted the boat and carried it down the hill. They waded across a pebbly beach until the sea was deep enough to launch the boat. Tom and Elenna scrambled aboard. Silver whined and tried to follow.

"No, boy," Elenna said, ruffling the thick fur around his neck. "You can't come this time."

"I'll look after him," Calum promised. "And your horse, too."

He rested his hand on Silver's head. The wolf looked up at him and let out a yelp good-bye.

"We'll be back soon," Tom said reassuringly.

"Wait! I want you to have this," Calum said, presenting his pearl-handled knife. "You found it, after all," Calum replied.

"We can't take this," Elenna said. "It belongs to your family."

"Then borrow it," Calum said, smiling.

"Thanks," Tom said, passing it to Elenna for safekeeping. We'll take good care of it."

Elenna gave Silver a last pat. Then she unlashed the oars and gave one to Tom. They began rowing out to sea. Back on the beach, Tom could still see Calum standing knee-deep in water, with Silver at his side.

Calum raised a hand to wave. "Good luck!" he called.

Tom waved back. Then, looking at Elenna, he muttered, "We're going to need it."

━→ CHAPTER SIX ←━

DISCOVERY ON THE ISLAND

Rowing was hard work. Sweat plastered Tom's tunic to his body. His hands ached from gripping the oar. Elenna's hair clung to her face and she snatched a moment to wipe her forehead with her sleeve.

An eerie silence hung around them. The only sounds were the creaking of the boat and their oars dipping into the water. As they rowed toward the island, the sea became choppy and a current seized the boat. It grew harder to make progress.

Tom's muscles strained as he dug the oars deeper into the restless sea. He squeezed his eyes shut and tried to concentrate on the task of rowing. He could hear Elenna huffing with effort, too.

Gradually the shape of a rocky islet began to poke through the misty dawn. "There it is," he told Elenna. "I think that's where I saw Sepron, just before the flood."

He looked over his shoulder, peering into the heavy fog. There was no sign of the sea serpent. Tom felt an icy shiver run down his spine as he thought of the great head rising out of the water.

Then Elenna let out a cry. "Tom! The boat's leaking!"

Tom started. Water was slowly filling the bottom of the boat. It was seeping in around the edges of the repair and began to pool near their feet.

"The tar must have been weakened by the water when we put out the fire," Elenna said.

"Give me your oar," Tom said. "I'll row while you bail. We'll try to find a place where we can land on the rocks."

Tom began to row again while Elenna used his shield to bail out the water.

The rocky islet gradually grew closer. But this islet had no beach — only rocky crags rising straight out of the sea.

The water swirled around the rocks as Tom angled the boat around them, struggling to keep it on a steady course.

"Careful, Tom!" Elenna shouted. "The waves could smash this boat to pieces on those rocks!"

Elenna was right. The boat lurched and rocked dangerously. They had to get away from the island. Tom started rowing back out to sea, when he spotted an iron hoop driven into a huge crag.

"Hey!" he called to Elenna. "Look at that!"

Tom saw that a thick, gold chain was fixed to it, leading down into the water. It was draped with seaweed and covered with barnacles, but it still gave off a mysterious golden glow.

Elenna caught her breath. "Do you think it's enchanted?"

"Only one way to find out!" he said.

Tom carefully navigated the boat back toward the island. He put down the oars and reached for the chain. The golden light felt alive, somehow, as if the chain were buzzing with energy.

"Think the serpent's got a leash?" Tom asked, smiling warily. He gave the chain a tug. It was surprisingly light for its size.

"No!" cried Elenna. "What if you wake Sepron?"

"It doesn't feel attached to anything below," Tom said as he began to pull the chain up.

As he said this, the chain came to the surface. It was broken! The last link was mangled and destroyed. All of a sudden, the churning waves died down and the water was calm again.

"Oh!" cried Elenna.

But Tom wasn't surprised. "Looks like Sepron is on the loose."

⊷ CHAPTER SEVEN ⊷

SEPRON AT LAST!

TOM SCANNED THE HORIZON FOR SIGNS OF Sepron, but saw only tranquil seas. By now the sun must have risen over the hills. But the sea mist had grown thicker still — the shore was blotted out. And everything was eerily quiet.

Elenna broke the silence. "I think the leak is getting worse. I can't bail fast enough."

"But there's nowhere to land the boat!" Tom said. "What can we do?"

"Quick!" Elenna shouted, ripping the bottom of her tunic. "Give me some cloth."

Tom ripped off his sleeve and handed it to Elenna.

"Hold the boat steady, Tom," she said. "I've got to plug the hole from underneath." With that, she jumped overboard into the frigid sea and disappeared under the surface. Tom tried to bail the water, but it was coming in too quickly.

I hope this works, thought Tom as he watched the water rise over his ankles. He felt panic seize him as water begin to fill the bottom of the hull. Just when he thought they were doomed, the water slowed, and then stopped almost entirely. He heard Elenna gasp as she came to the surface.

"You did it," Tom exclaimed as he helped pull Elenna back into the boat.

"It will help," she said, "but it won't completely stop the flow. And it won't hold for long." Tom continued to bail out the water with his shield as Elenna tried to warm up. She was shivering and her lips were blue with cold.

"Here," Tom said, handing her his coat.

As the boat bobbed gently on the sea, the mist

began to thicken. It wrapped around them like a cold, wet blanket. Soon, they couldn't see farther than a few feet away. An eerie silence descended upon them.

"We'd better start rowing again," Tom said.

"But we don't know which way to go," Elenna said, shivering. She was right. Sepron could be anywhere — he hadn't shown up on the map since the day before.

Elenna leaned over the edge of the boat, trying to peer through the fog. Just then the boat rocked wildly, almost sending her overboard.

She jumped back to her seat. "What was that?" she asked, her voice shaking with fear.

Tom summoned all his courage and looked down into the water.

"There's something there!" he exclaimed. "Something huge."

Sure enough, a vast dark shadow was gliding underneath the boat. Then he froze at the sound of loud splashing. Something had broken through the surface of the water on the other side. Huge drops of seawater rained down on him and Elenna.

Tom knew what he was going to see. Bracing himself, he grabbed for his sword and shield, and glanced over his shoulder. Elenna screamed.

Rearing out of the sea was the huge head of the sea monster. At last Tom was face-to-face with Sepron!

The serpent's eyes flashed with an icy glare of anger. Shimmering scales, the color of the sea, covered his head and neck. Barnacles and seaweed clung to him, and the water foamed around him where he broke the surface.

"Look at that," Tom said, pointing. "The lock is the same as Ferno the Fire Dragon's."

The beast's collar was locked with a huge padlock, and the broken golden chain trailed from it.

Roaring, Sepron lashed his head to and fro in agitation. Then he plunged back under the waves.

The surface of the sea rolled as he vanished, and the boat rocked dangerously. Tom peered down into the sea. He narrowed his eyes as an idea grew inside him. Sepron was down there, somewhere. But the serpent couldn't hide forever. Tom knew what he had to do. He had to follow him.

They rowed around the rocks and then out into the open water, following in his wake. Elenna put all her effort into rowing. Tom could feel the cold fist of fear in the pit of his stomach. He could see that Elenna was scared, too.

"I'm going in." he said. "If I can hold my breath for long enough, I should be able to unlock the collar with the key Aduro gave me and break the spell." He pulled it out from under his shirt and held it up.

Elenna gave him an anxious look, but didn't try to stop him. "Be careful," she said quietly.

"Don't worry, I will."

"There must be something I can do to help," Elenna said.

"Here," Tom replied, handing Elenna his sword. "In case something happens."

Tom slipped off his boots and tucked the key away safely, before climbing over the side of the boat. Time almost stood still as he took a huge gulp of air. Then he dove into the icy water.

CHAPTER EIGHT

SEPRON'S KINGDOM

TOM STRUCK OUT ENERGETICALLY, DIVING deeper into the sea. He was swimming in an eerie world, where everything seemed to move more slowly. As he swam down, the water became darker and colder. Silver bubbles of air streamed away from his mouth, rising to the surface.

As he plunged deeper, the only sound was the rushing in his ears. Fear gripped him as he faced the dark depths. He would never be able to hold his breath long enough. He turned around and swam back to the surface, gasping for air.

He forced himself to be calm. He couldn't turn

back now. This was his quest. No one else could help the fishermen and free the Kingdom of Avantia from the threat of Sepron. Tom had to succeed. He plunged back down, diving deeper still with strong, sure strokes.

Tom saw a flash of shimmering scales in the murky waters below—he knew he must be close. He continued to dive down until he spotted a reef of coral near the seabed. Lying among the coral was Sepron.

Tom froze and almost took a huge gulp of water. Sepron's head and the collar with the padlock were closest to him. The sea serpent's body stretched away into the darkness.

As Tom swam closer, the huge head swung around. The Beast's jaws gaped open, revealing vicious rows of teeth. Sepron surged up through the water, heading straight for Tom.

Tom turned back. Arms and legs pumping, he

swam up to the surface. The last of his air bubbled away. His lungs were hurting as he fought not to breathe in any water.

He glanced back, engulfed by the fear that Sepron's mighty jaws would clamp down on his legs. The sea monster followed closely behind Tom, snapping his jaws open and shut. It was as if the serpent was taunting him.

A moment later, Tom's head and shoulders broke the surface. He treaded water, desperately gulping in air. Looking around for the boat, he couldn't see anything through the thick fog.

Tom kept treading water, calling out for his friend. *Where was Elenna?* Then, he heard a faint cry.

"Tom! Are you all right?" Elenna called out.

Tom looked all around, and then he saw it, a glint of silver not too far away. He swam toward the sparkling light. It was Elenna, holding Tom's sword.

"Yes," Tom panted. He felt exhausted. But he

knew he had to go back. He dragged his limbs through the water over to Elenna and the boat. Could he really dive down there again? "I have to!" he muttered to himself as he swam.

"Did you free Sepron?" Elenna asked, pulling him into the boat. Tom shook his head and tried to ignore the bitter stab of disappointment as he admitted that he'd failed.

"Found him, but —" Tom was still gasping for air. "Couldn't get close enough. Got to try again."

"Don't take in too much air," Elenna advised. "And try to move slowly so you don't waste it."

He rested until he had caught his breath. Then he took a last gulp of air and plunged beneath the surface.

This time he found the reef quickly. Sepron was lying there again, his coils wrapped loosely around a spire of coral.

Cautiously, Tom swam closer, keeping behind a rock wall until he could approach Sepron from behind. He slid through the water, desperate not to alert the serpent of his presence. At last he could grasp the glowing collar in one hand.

Right away, Sepron knew Tom was there. He lashed his head back and forth, trying to shake him off. Tom clung on and worked his way around until he was under Sepron's jutting jaws. He grabbed the padlock that lay against the serpent's thick, rough scales.

As quickly as he could, Tom took Wizard Aduro's key from his pocket. He tried to thrust it into the hole in the padlock. But the hole was encrusted with barnacles. Numb with horror, Tom realized the key was useless until he could clear the keyhole.

Just then, Sepron's head heaved upward. Tom lost his grip on the padlock and rolled over helplessly in the surging water. One of the serpent's coils knocked Tom from behind, and he felt the air go out of him. He had to surface or he would drown!

⇥ Chapter Nine ⇤

THE LAST CHANCE

Sepron's neck curved around. His hungry jaws reached for Tom. With failing strength, Tom kicked out, driving himself back to the surface. His chest was bursting for more air.

As he surfaced, he spotted the glint of sunlight from the sword Elenna held. Shaking wet hair out of his eyes, he gulped lungfuls of air.

"Tom!" Elenna cried. "Is everything all right?"

"No. The keyhole is blocked by barnacles." Tom's voice was hoarse. He swam up to the boat and grabbed the side. "There's no way to get the collar off."

Elenna's eyes widened in horror. "What are we going to do?" Then, before Tom could reply, she exclaimed, "I know!" She fished in her pocket until she brought out Calum's knife.

Tom brightened at the sight of the intricate knife. Its pearl handle seemed to glow.

"I'll give it a try," he said.

Elenna handed him the blade. Then Tom plunged down into the sea again. A massive shadow fell over him, and he realized that Sepron was waiting for him.

The serpent's neck arched over Tom. Sepron's sharp teeth closed inches from Tom's foot as he swam deeper. Tom knew he couldn't outswim the Beast. He had to unfasten the collar!

His heart thumping, Tom knew he had to act now. His air wouldn't last long, and if he tried to resurface, Sepron would snap him up. *This is my last chance!* he thought.

He turned in the water and drove himself toward Sepron's body. As the huge jaws gaped open, Tom swam underneath and grabbed the padlock. Sepron's scaly head lashed to and fro. Tom jabbed the knife into the keyhole, scraping at the barnacles. It was hard work, but at last he had cleared the hole.

By now he needed air again. His arms and legs were heavy with exhaustion and his wet clothes were dragging him down.

Summoning all his strength, he shoved the key into the lock and turned it. *This has to work!* he told himself.

The lock sprang open. Instantly, Sepron stopped thrashing about. He tossed his head, and the collar came off, floating down to the sea floor. For so long now, Sepron had been under the evil spell of Malvel. But not anymore. With fierce determination, he tore the golden chain apart with his teeth.

Tom watched in wonder as the collar sank and the golden glow faded into the depths of the sea.

He couldn't believe it. Sepron was free at last!

CHAPTER TEN

THE NEXT QUEST

TOM MADE HIS WAY TOWARD THE SURFACE. His head swam with exhaustion and he could hardly make his arms and legs move.

Then he felt something nudge him from below. Terror gripped him as he looked down into Sepron's face. But the anger that was there before had gone. The serpent's eyes seemed kind. He gave Tom another nudge with his rough muzzle, pushing him up toward the light.

As Tom broke the surface, Sepron lifted him out of the water. Tom clung to the Beast's muzzle as he stretched his neck out toward the boat.

"Tom!" Elenna cried out. "The collar's gone. You did it!"

Tom looked up. "Yes. He's free now."

As the sea serpent lowered his head to set Tom down gently in the boat, something fell from his jaws. Tom picked it up.

"It's a tooth," he said, gazing at the jagged piece of ivory. *Sepron must have broken it,* he realized, *when he tore at the collar.*

Tom reached up a hand and touched the Beast's shimmering scales. "Thank you," he said. He knew that without Sepron's help, he would have drowned.

The Beast dipped his head in farewell. Then he dove back under the surface. Tom caught a glimpse of him gliding away toward the open sea. It was beautiful to see how gracefully Sepron moved through the waves — truly at home.

"Sepron's free now," he said. "I think it's safe to say that there won't be any more floods."

He and Elenna stared at each other. Then Elenna let out a whoop of triumph. She and Tom flung their arms around each other and hugged in excitement and relief.

Tom started at the sound of a polite cough just behind him. He and Elenna leaped apart. Tom turned to see Aduro. He seemed to be standing on the waves close to the boat. Tom could see the blue ocean through his robes and realized this was another one of the wizard's illusions. After all they had been through, it was good to see a friendly face.

"Well done!" the wizard said. "I can see I was right when I chose you, Tom. You've saved Avantia from Sepron."

"I couldn't have done it without Elenna," said Tom.

Aduro smiled. "You have both shown great courage," he said. "All of Avantia will be grateful to you. And now," he added, "is that Sepron's tooth that I see there?"

Tom held out the jagged piece. "I think it broke when he tore his chain off."

"Place it in the front of your shield," the wizard instructed him.

Tom did as Aduro told him. Another empty slot had opened up beside the scale of Ferno the Fire Dragon. Sea-green light spilled out of it. It glowed brightly as Tom fitted Sepron's tooth into the hole. Then the sides of the hole closed around the tooth as if the shield had been waiting for it all along.

"Now as long as you hold your shield, you will never drown," Aduro said, "and not even the fiercest torrent will be able to harm you."

Tom gazed at the shield in wonder. He had already tested it against fire. Now it would protect him from water as well. "Thank you!" he said.

"Don't thank me," said Aduro, his eyes twinkling. "You won the tooth yourself. With each Beast that you help, your powers will grow."

Tom glanced at Elenna, whose eyes were wide with wonder.

"What must we do now?" she asked.

"First, go back to the village," replied the wizard. "I'll see that Elenna's repair holds until you reach the shore. You have a boat to return."

Tom nodded. "Yes, and we have to collect Storm and Silver."

"Then you must ride to the mountains in the North," Aduro went on. "Cypher the Giant is threatening the kingdom."

"What's happening?" Elenna asked.

"The Dark Wizard Malvel has put a spell on the giant," the wizard replied. "In his anger, Cypher is sending avalanches down on the trading route at the foot of the mountains. Without these important routes, the whole Kingdom will suffer."

"And it's our job to stop him," Tom said. He could imagine rocks and earth raining down, and the terror of the townspeople.

"That's right," said Aduro. "Freeing Cypher is your next quest."

"I'll do my best," Tom promised.

"The map will help guide you," the wizard told him.

"Thank you. I —" Tom began. But as he was speaking, Aduro's form began to fade. The ocean shone more brightly through his robes. Then he was gone.

Tom gazed toward the shore. Amazingly, despite all they had been through, little time had passed. Hopefully, the villagers were still sleeping and no one but Calum would guess what he had done.

"The fishermen will be fine now," Elenna said with satisfaction.

Tom nodded. With Sepron freed, the fish would

return, and the villagers would soon repair the damage of the flood.

He felt a sudden pang of loneliness for his uncle and aunt, and even the father he'd never known. But he knew it was his fate to carry on with his quest.

Tom and Elenna rowed back to the beach. Silver was dashing up and down at the water's edge, yelping excitedly. When Elenna reached him, he flung himself at her. He rested his paws on her shoulders and licked her face.

Elenna put her arms around him, plunging her hands into his thick fur. "Oh, Silver, I'm glad to be back!" she cried.

Calum appeared, leading Storm, as Tom pulled the boat up onto the beach. Tom leaned against the horse and stroked his silky forelock.

Storm nuzzled his shoulder and blew out a warm breath as if he was welcoming Tom back. Tom's loneliness suddenly vanished. He wouldn't see his uncle and aunt for a long time, but he had a new family now: Elenna and Silver and Storm. With the three of them by his side, he knew that he would have the strength to face Cypher the Giant.

"I could see the serpent from the ridge," Calum said, pointing uphill. "I was worried you wouldn't make it back." He reached out and gripped Tom's hand.

"If it wasn't for your knife, we wouldn't have," Tom said, pulling the knife from his belt. He held it out to Calum. But Calum refused to take it.

"Keep it," Calum said with a nod. "You may need it again."

"Thank you, my friend," Tom said gratefully. "Your kindness will not be forgotten."

"Nor will your courage," said Calum.

Tom turned his gaze to the North. Somewhere

in the distance, he knew, Cypher the Giant was hurling rocks down a mountainside. It was Tom's task to free him from the evil spell. That was his next quest. And whatever the danger, he would face it with his friends beside him.